D0047312

my LiTTLE
PONY
PONYVILLE MYSTERIES

Journey to the Livewood

by Penumbra Quill

Little, Brown and Company
New York Boston

This book is a work of fiction. Names, characters, places, and incidents are the product of the author's imagination or are used fictitiously. Any resemblance to actual events, locales, or persons, living or dead, is coincidental.

Cover design by Christina Quintero. Cover illustration by Franco Spagnolo.

Little, Brown and Company
Hachette Book Group
1290 Avenue of the Americas, New York, NY 10104
Visit us at LBYR.com
mylittlepony.com

First Edition: June 2018

Little, Brown and Company is a division of Hachette Book Group, Inc. The Little, Brown name and logo are trademarks of Hachette Book Group, Inc.

The publisher is not responsible for websites (or their content) that are not owned by the publisher.

Library of Congress Control Number 2017964060

ISBNs: 978-0-316-47576-1 (pbk.), 978-0-316-47575-4 (ebook)

Printed in the United States of America

LSC-C

10 9 8 7 6 5 4 3 2 1

CHAPTER ONE

Apple Bloom scrunched even lower in her hiding spot, gripping Nightmare Moon's helm close to her chest. On the other side of the tree, she could hear hoofsteps stalking closer. Apple Bloom held her breath, muscles tensed. For as long as she could remember, she'd wanted to be a hero like her sister, Applejack—facing down fearsome beasts, overcoming impossible odds, saving the day when all hope was lost. It was finally the Cutie Mark Crusaders' chance to prove they were as brave and capable as their big sisters and friends... and Apple Bloom couldn't wait to show Applejack and everypony else that they had what it took to save Equestria!

A blast of magenta magic sizzled over

Apple Bloom's hiding spot. No time for daydreaming now—she had to move! With a bounce and a twist, she leaped out from behind the tree just as another arc of Unicorn magic shot past her heels.

"Now, Scootaloo!" Apple Bloom hollered as she bucked Nightmare Moon's helm in a high arc over her pursuer's head. Scootaloo, perched in a tree above, her helmet on and scooter at the ready, zoomed down a branch and intercepted the helm in midair. Their attacker turned her magic on Scootaloo, but the light-green shimmer of Sweetie Belle's shield protected the Pegasus from the incoming blast.

"Hurry!" Sweetie Belle shrilled. Scootaloo landed her scooter and hurled the helm to Apple Bloom again. Apple Bloom leaped to catch it. It looked like they were going to pull this off!

And then suddenly, vines glowing with magic tangled around her hooves, trapping her. Sweetie Belle and Scootaloo rushed in to help, but as they struggled to tug Apple Bloom loose, the vines wrapped around them, too!

"We can't... give up!" Apple Bloom cried as all three thrashed desperately to get free. It was too late. Nightmare Moon's helm flew from Apple Bloom's grasp, then levitated away. The vines went slack, and the three defeated Crusaders turned to face...

Twilight Sparkle. Apple Bloom could tell the helpful Alicorn was trying to stay positive, but clearly their hero training was not going as well as she'd hoped.

"Let's... try that again," Twilight said with false cheer.

"Hadn't they better rest a bit first?" Rarity asked with concern as she moved to help up the Crusaders. Apple Bloom saw Sweetie Belle roll her eyes as Rarity produced a brush from somewhere and began pulling it through her little sister's mane. "Honestly, Twilight Sparkle, you'll exhaust them before they even *see* Auntie Eclipse."

"Better tired than unprepared," Applejack said, and Apple Bloom had to agree with her sister. They wanted to be ready for whatever terrifying things the wicked sorceress Auntie Eclipse threw at them. So far, those had included a bogle, Timberwolves, the Olden Pony, and a bad-luck curse. And Apple Bloom was sure the wicked Unicorn had more nastiness planned.

"Yeah! You should see how many times we practice our moves before a Wonderbolts show!" Rainbow Dash said as she flew in to grab "Nightmare Moon's helm"—really just a trash can they were using as a prop—and put it back behind the tree on a pedestal.

"Okay, Blue Moon, we're ready for round fifty-seven!"

Apple Bloom glanced over at Blue Moon, who stood at the edge of their training clearing. It was strange to see him without his signature creepy smile, but now Apple Bloom knew that had just been part of the spell Auntie Eclipse used to make him do her evil bidding. The same spell that the CMCs' friends Lilymoon and Ambermoon were now under. Auntie Eclipse was probably forcing them and their mother, Lumi Nation, to use their matching cutie marks to open the Livewood at this very moment. Then, Auntie would steal the helm of Nightmare Moon from the secret place Princesses Luna and Celestia had hidden it, and she would use it to bring all of Equestria under her rule, and then...

"Apple Bloom? Sugarcube? Ya sure

you're up ta all this?" Applejack frowned with concern. "It's not too late ta back out. I know y'all must be scared. Why don'tcha let Twilight and the rest of us grown ponies handle things instead?"

Apple Bloom sighed—even though Princess Luna *herself* had said that the CMCs were the only ones who could protect the Livewood, and even though they'd proven themselves time and time again, her sister *still* wanted to make her sit on the sidelines. Well, Apple Bloom wasn't a tiny filly anymore! She was a hero! Or . . . would be. Soon.

"Nope!" Apple Bloom said stubbornly. "Fire up the time pocket, Blue Moon!" The Unicorn nodded. Magic bloomed around his horn, and he pointed it at a small golden pendant decorated with a clock face picked out in rubies.

The strange magical artifact belonged to Auntie Eclipse. She had given it to Blue Moon while he was under her spell, but now that he was free of her control, he was using it to help the Cutie Mark Crusaders. The time pocket, which Rainbow Dash had nicknamed the "ultimate do-over," had the power to turn back time in a small area—about the size of the clearing—for one minute. This allowed a pony to fix a mistake or just keep reliving the same minute again and again—as the Crusaders were doing now. Twilight's plan was that if they practiced enough training scenarios, they'd be ready for whatever Auntie threw at the CMCs—and they wouldn't lose any time preparing.

As the time pocket activated, everything in the clearing seemed to move backward, blurring as ghost images of Twilight and the Crusaders flitted back to their original starting positions. Apple Bloom grabbed the trash-can helm with determination. She'd make Applejack see that the Cutie Mark Crusaders could handle whatever the Livewood held!

CHAPTER TWO

"Did ya remember your hoofwarmers? How 'bout a scarf? A jug of water? A *backup* jug of water, in case that one leaks?" Applejack quizzed Apple Bloom as they waited at the edge of the Everfree Forest for Scootaloo to join the rest of the assembled ponies.

Apple Bloom shifted the bag across her shoulder and tried to stay patient. She knew Applejack's nagging was just the way she showed she cared, but it was getting really tiring. Couldn't she just trust that Apple Bloom knew how to pack for an adventure? A glance over to Sweetie Belle made her realize that overprotectiveness wasn't just an Apple trait. Rarity was fussing over her little sister, too.

"*Why* would I need hoof polish to go into the Livewood?" Sweetie Belle exclaimed in frustration as Rarity selected a bottle of candy-apple-red lacquer. "I'm trying to stop Auntie Eclipse, not dance at the Grand Galloping Gala."

"That's no excuse for not looking your best!" Rarity sniffed. But she put away the polish.

"Finally! What took you so long?" An impatient Rainbow Dash greeted Scootaloo as the young Pegasus raced up on her scooter. Oddly, a lumpy blanket with cartoony Daring Do cutouts sewn on it and a large bag that smelled like snickerdoodles weighed her down.

"Sorry," Scootaloo puffed. "Aunt Holiday baked us 'Save Equestria' cookies, and Auntie Lofty sewed me a hero quilt. They're great, but kinda heavy."

Apple Bloom looked wistfully at the cookies. Why couldn't Applejack show she cared like *that*—with baked goods?

"We can put them with the rest of our things." Twilight smiled, magically lifting the quilt and cookies from Scootaloo and folding them neatly into a wagon with the group's supplies. She faced the gathered ponies—Pinkie Pie, Fluttershy, Rainbow Dash, Applejack, Rarity, Starlight Glimmer, Blue Moon, and the Cutie Mark Crusaders.

"A great danger faces our world. But I have no doubt that these three ponies have the courage and friendship to protect Nightmare Moon's helm from falling into the wrong hooves."

Apple Bloom's heart swelled with pride. The Princess of Friendship believing in them almost made up for Applejack's doubt. Almost. Nearby, Sweetie Belle stood taller, and Scootaloo grinned.

"While they do that, it's up to us to keep them safe," Twilight continued. "So if everypony is ready?" Apple Bloom watched as the others agreed—and even though Applejack looked like she was sucking on a crab apple while she did it, she nodded, too.

Twilight turned and led the way into the Everfree Forest.

In the daytime, the long journey to the Livewood didn't seem to take *nearly* as long. *Probably because Twilight knows exactly where she's going*, Apple Bloom thought.

"Remember what I told y'all," Applejack said, giving advice for what had to be the hundred and twenty-second time, "if things get too dangerous, you three get out of there faster than a pickle barrel on a grease chute, ya hear?"

The other Crusaders smiled at Applejack's turn of phrase, but Apple Bloom had had just about enough of her sister's bossiness.

"Lets get going, y'all. Didn't we have those

questions we wanted to ask Blue Moon about Auntie's magic?" They didn't really have any questions, but surely talking to the Unicorn would be better than being reminded to wipe their noses and keep their hooves clean, Apple Bloom thought. The other Crusaders picked up on her signal, and they nodded vigorously.

The CMCs moved down the line of ponies to walk with Blue Moon. He gave them a small, sad smile.

"I'm sorry you three have to go through all this. I wish we'd never moved to Ponyville. If only Lumi and I had been able to stop Auntie Eclipse sooner."

"It's not your fault," Sweetie Belle said. "You were just trying to keep your family safe."

"And we're really glad you *did* move here," Scootaloo said. "Otherwise, we'd never have met Ambermoon and Lilymoon."

"We'll make everythin' right," Apple Bloom reassured Blue Moon.

"You know, I believe you will," Blue Moon said. "You've foiled Auntie's plans more than anypony I know. She views you as a true threat to her success. But remember, she is ruthless. She will do whatever it takes to achieve her final goal—to possess the helm."

"That . . . doesn't sound very encouraging," Scootaloo pointed out.

"Maybe not—but her focus is also her flaw," Blue Moon explained. "Sometimes Auntie's drive is so all-consuming, it makes her blind to everything else. And that leaves you a way to sneak past her guard. Pay attention—you probably won't get more than one chance to trip her up."

"Thanks for the advice, Blue Moon. Sorry we thought you were a baddie, too," blurted

Apple Bloom. Surprisingly, Blue Moon laughed.

"I would've thought the same thing in your horseshoes," he said. "I can see why my daughters have found such true friends in you three."

An eerie howl cut through the air, the sound tracing an invisible claw down Apple Bloom's spine. She shivered. By now, the Crusaders knew that noise well.

"Timberwolf," Sweetie Belle whispered, her eyes wide. A chorus of howls answered the first, climbing up and down the scale in fiendish glee.

"Timber*wolves*," Scootaloo corrected.

Apple Bloom gulped. That meant they were getting close to the Livewood.

CHAPTER THREE

Although it was the middle of the day, the clearing around the Livewood still seemed somehow darker than the rest of the Forest. Three large pillars stood like silent guardians facing the twisting wall of vines that prevented anypony from entering the heart of the wood.

Apple Bloom looked around for any sign of Auntie Eclipse, but everything in the clearing seemed exactly like it had the last time they were here.

"It's still closed." Scootaloo turned to the rest of the ponies, looking hopeful. "Maybe Auntie Eclipse couldn't get in?"

Sweetie Belle shook her head. "Listen," she whispered. Everypony went quiet. Apple Bloom strained her ears, trying to figure out what she was supposed to be listening for.

“I don’t hear nothin’,” Apple Bloom finally whispered back.

“Exactly,” Sweetie Belle said. “No snarling and growling *inside* the Livewood. The Timberwolves are all roaming the Forest. I bet they got out when Auntie Eclipse and the others went in.”

“Then there’s no time to lose,” Twilight said firmly. She nodded toward the pillars. “Let’s get you three up there and see if this ‘matching cutie mark’ key works.”

Apple Bloom glanced at her friends. Scootaloo looked determined. Sweetie Belle seemed like she was going to be sick. But they both turned to Apple Bloom and nodded. They were ready. Each of the Crusaders chose a different pillar and began walking up the steps that were carved naturally into the earth, vines, and rock.

“Careful now!” Applejack called out.

Apple Bloom blew out a frustrated breath. She was about to go stop an ancient witch from getting the most dangerous magical artifact in Equestria, and her sister was worried she was gonna slip? Why couldn't she—

Apple Bloom tripped on a vine.

"What did I just say?" Applejack called from below.

"If you would let me walk up here in peace, I wouldn'ta tripped!" Apple Bloom snapped back.

"She does have a point," Apple Bloom heard Starlight say. Recovering her balance, Apple Bloom hurried the rest of the way up. Sweetie Belle and Scootaloo were already standing atop their pillars.

"Whoa!" Rainbow Dash said, hovering near the pillars. Apple Bloom looked to see what had surprised Rainbow Dash. Scootaloo's and Sweetie Belle's cutie marks were glowing brightly!

"Ouch!" Apple Bloom yelped. Her flank was burning! She turned and saw that her cutie mark was glowing as well. The pain quickly subsided, and Apple Bloom looked hopefully at the Livewood. Their matching cutie marks had worked—the twisting vines were untangling and pulling back from one another! Apple Bloom could make out a small stone structure in the shadows with stairs that led down into the earth below.

The Livewood was open.

"I *think* you can come down now," Twilight called up to them. Apple Bloom, Scootaloo, and Sweetie Belle rushed down to join the others, who were moving to investigate the Livewood's entrance.

"Now that it's open, why can't we all go in together? No reason for them to have to do this alone," Applejack said.

"I concur," Rarity said as she studied the ominous stairs inside.

"We can make it a Save Equestria party!" Pinkie shouted as she tried to rush into the Livewood. Several vines shot out and blocked her. Pinkie dodged to the right, but more vines moved to intercept her. Pinkie started giggling. "I've never played tag with vines before. Who knew they were so good?"

"Apple Bloom, over here," Twilight beckoned as she watched the vines block Pinkie Pie. Apple Bloom moved to stand next to Twilight, and the Alicorn nodded toward the opening the vines had made. "You try." Apple Bloom could see Applejack nervously step toward her, but Fluttershy placed a hoof on her friend's shoulder, and Applejack stayed put. Apple Bloom took a few cautious steps, expecting the vines to whip out and stop her as well, but nothing happened. She looked ahead at the stairs and kept moving steadily toward them, sure any second that something or somepony was going to leap out and stop her.

When she put her hoof down on the first step, she turned and looked back to see everypony staring at her. Twilight nodded grimly.

"I thought so," Twilight said. "Only they can go in. I guess that settles it."

"But what about Auntie Eclipse?" Sweetie Belle asked. "She didn't have a matching cutie mark. Do you think she couldn't get in, either?"

"I doubt we're that lucky." Twilight turned to Sweetie Belle with a nervous smile. "You'll find out before we do." Apple Bloom was pretty certain Auntie Eclipse was down there. She also figured the old witch knew they were coming in after her, and that she'd have something nasty planned to stop them. Still, the Crusaders had a job to do.

"Well?" Apple Bloom called to Sweetie Belle and Scootaloo. "Let's shake a hoof, y'all. We've got Equestria to save!"

"Wait a moment!" Blue Moon reached out a hoof to stop Scootaloo. He passed her the time pocket artifact. "In case you run into any danger, a 'do-over' might be useful." Scootaloo nodded her thanks, slipping the magic device into her satchel.

"You've all got this. You're ready," said Twilight. Starlight nodded in agreement.

"Be *very* careful," Fluttershy cautioned.

"Don't touch anything that looks at all dangerous!" Rarity cried.

"Don't do *anything* I would normally do!" Rainbow Dash stressed.

"Have *fun*!" Pinkie announced, still dodging the vines. *"Wheeeeeee!"*

Apple Bloom looked back at her sister, expecting her to say something really annoying.

"I love you, sis," Applejack said, worry clearly etched on her face. Apple Bloom was about to say she would be fine, but she felt a lump in her throat and just nodded. Then the Crusaders turned and walked down the stairs into the unknown depths below.

CHAPTER FOUR

"How far do these steps *go*?" Scootaloo groaned. "We've been walking *forever*!" The steps just kept going down, down, down, deeper than Apple Bloom thought possible. At first Sweetie Belle's horn had been their only source of light, but as they moved farther down the corridor, they discovered a strange glowing purple moss growing on the walls that allowed them to see farther. Not that there was much *to* see. Just more steps.

"So once we *do* find Auntie Eclipse and the others... what exactly are we planning to do?" Sweetie Belle asked in what Apple Bloom knew was her "trying to sound casual" voice.

"We'll figure it out," Apple Bloom stated. "We always have before!"

"But every other time there was *some*pony helping us," Scootaloo pointed out. "We had Lilymoon explaining some kind of magical creature, and Zecora giving us a potion, and Starlight protecting us, and Discord... being super weird and Discord-y."

"Yeah, but actually takin' care of the problem was up to *us*," Apple Bloom insisted, getting annoyed. "You heard Blue Moon! We've messed up Auntie Eclipse's plans more than anypony, and she's older than dirt! There's a reason *we* were chosen to open the Livewood."

"Uh. Yeah... and I think I found it," Sweetie Belle called back to them. Apple Bloom looked over and realized that they were *finally* at the end of the stairs! Sweetie Belle's hooves shuffled nervously on the bottom step, staring at something just out of their sight. Apple Bloom hurried down to join her.

The base of the staircase faced a cavernous passageway. It looked a little like the halls in the palace in Canterlot, Apple Bloom thought, but older, danker, and covered in more of the glowing purple moss. There were at least fifty arched doorways leading off in different directions. Apple Bloom had no idea how they were going to figure out which one to take.

"What is *that*?" Scootaloo asked loudly. Apple Bloom turned to see what her friends were looking at and gasped.

High on a sidewall was a *huge* drawing of...the Cutie Mark Crusaders? Apple Bloom squinted to be sure. There were three ponies crudely drawn. An Earth pony with a bow in her mane, a Pegasus with tiny wings, and a Unicorn that looked—

"Why did they make me look so scared?" Sweetie Belle huffed indignantly. Scootaloo and Apple Bloom giggled.

"You make that face *all* the time," Scootaloo said, imitating the drawing of Sweetie Belle.

"But...who drew that?" Apple Bloom asked. "Princess Luna said that she didn't make the pillars—the peryton did. So why would there be a drawing of us on the wall all the way down here?"

"You don't think Smartyhoof drew it, do you?" Sweetie Belle asked dubiously.

"Or Ambermoon or Lilymoon!" said Scootaloo excitedly. "Maybe one of them broke free of Auntie Eclipse's spell!"

"And decided to draw us a picture?" Apple Bloom asked skeptically. "Why would they do that?"

"Maybe it's a clue!" suggested Sweetie Belle. The three Crusaders cocked their heads and studied the wall together. Apple Bloom realized that the three ponies in the drawing were pointing in different directions. The image of Apple Bloom was making a face like she smelled something funny and was pointing to the left. The image of Sweetie Belle *did* look scared and was pointing to the right. But Scootaloo was smiling widely and pointing straight up at the ceiling.

"What am I pointing at?" Scootaloo asked, clearly reaching the same conclusion Apple Bloom had. They all turned their heads to look up at the high vaulted ceiling above them.

"I think I see something!" Sweetie Belle breathed. "There, way high up!" Apple Bloom saw it, too. She walked farther into the room to get a better look.

"It's writin'!" she called to the others. They rushed over to help decipher it.

"S-T-A...stand! It says *stand*!" Scootaloo squinted as she tried to make it out.

"Stand there!" Apple Bloom said. "I think it means to stand right below it!" The Crusaders rushed over to stand directly beneath the writing.

"Now what?" Sweetie Belle wondered aloud. Suddenly they heard a grinding noise. The stone below them sunk into the ground. A block of stone *slammed* down from the arch, cutting off the way to the stairs that led back up. All around them, slabs of rock crashed down, blocking *all* the doors.

"That wasn't a clue!" Apple Bloom groaned. "It was a *trap*!"

CHAPTER FIVE

"Auntie Eclipse must have drawn those pictures to fool us into trapping ourselves!" Sweetie Belle wailed. *"I can't believe we fell for it!"* Apple Bloom couldn't believe it, either. So much for being great heroes. They hadn't even made it past the first room! Still, she couldn't give up—there was too much at stake here!

"Just hold on." Apple Bloom could hear the panic in her own voice, but she was trying to keep the others calm. "There's gotta be a way outta this!" Apple Bloom's mind raced to find a solution, but all she could think about was how far beneath the forest they were. With no way out!

"You guys are hilarious," Scootaloo said, sounding *way* too relaxed. Apple Bloom and

Sweetie Belle both turned to look at her. She reached into her satchel and pulled out the time pocket.

"Auntie Eclipse may think she's pretty smart," Scootaloo said, grinning, "But she doesn't know we have her time pocket. We can just back up a minute and avoid ever being trapped!"

"Oh, thank goodness." Sweetie Belle sighed, clearly relieved. Apple Bloom sighed as well. It looked like they were going to get another chance to be heroes after all. As soon as Sweetie Belle activated the time pocket with her horn, all those stone slabs would rise up and... Apple Bloom studied the slabs; there was something written *on* them. It looked like...

"There!" Sweetie Belle yelled, her horn glowing bright. Magical energy surrounded the time pocket.

"Wait!" Apple Bloom shouted, but it was too late. Everything blurred around them as they ghosted back to where they had been a minute before. They stood together in the archway at the bottom of the stairs.

"Take *that*, you old witch!" Scootaloo yelled out to the chamber. Apple Bloom rushed back to the center of the room.

"Careful!" Sweetie Belle yelled. "You don't wanna set off the trap again!"

"Actually, I *do*!" Apple Bloom said, searching the floor. "I think there was somethin' written on those stones that blocked the doors!"

"More of Auntie Eclipse's nasty tricks?" Scootaloo shrugged.

"Maybe...but I don't think so." *There!* Apple Bloom could see the spot on the floor that activated the trap. She turned to Scootaloo and Sweetie Belle. "I'm gonna stand here. When those stones fall down in fronta the doors, look at what's on 'em. We'll be quick, and if it *is* a trap, we can just use the time pocket again!" Scootaloo and Sweetie Belle didn't look thrilled, but they nodded. Apple Bloom pressed her hoof on the floor, and it sunk down again. The massive stones dropped in front of the doors, same as before. The Crusaders studied the rock slabs.

"Look!" Sweetie Belle pointed. "It's an arrow!" Sure enough, there was an arrow scrawled on one of the stones blocking a doorway.

"Here, too!" Scootaloo called. In fact, *every* rock in front of a door had an arrow scrawled on it. And they were all pointing in the same direction. The Crusaders rushed through the large room, following the arrows.

"If we don't use the time pocket soon, we'll be stuck here," Sweetie Belle warned.

"I got a good feelin' about this," Apple Bloom called back. She looked up ahead. The next set of stone blocks had arrows in the opposite direction, all pointing back the way they had come. Whatever the arrows were pointing at must be right where they were standing!

"Well?" Scootaloo asked, agitated. Apple Bloom searched around frantically.

"Only a few seconds left!" Sweetie Belle was already powering up her horn, ready to activate the magical artifact.

"There! What's that?" Apple Bloom pointed to a crack on the wall across the hall from them. Something was lodged inside. Apple Bloom rushed over and tugged at the object. It was a tiny, plain wooden box. Nothing special about it. She shook it. She heard bells jingling faintly inside. Where had she heard those before?

"Apple Bloom!" Sweetie Belle was ready to activate the time pocket. But Apple Bloom suddenly realized why the bells were familiar. She threw the box to the ground.

There was a bright flash of light, and the sound of dozens of chiming bells filled the chamber.

"Smartyhoof!" Sweetie Belle called in delight, powering down her horn. Scootaloo cheered. Apple Bloom grinned. They had found the peryton!

CHAPTER SIX

The peryton dipped its antlers and stretched its shadowy wings wide. Watching the half stag, half eagle cavort around the room, Apple Bloom could tell it was happy to be free.

"But what were you doing in that tiny box?" Sweetie Belle asked.

The peryton tossed its head angrily and stomped its front hooves, chiming an answer that Apple Bloom didn't understand but could tell sounded angry.

"Did somepony trap you in there?" asked Sweetie Belle, her eyes wide.

"I bet it was Auntie Eclipse!" Scootaloo frowned. Even Apple Bloom thought the peryton's jingled response sounded like a yes.

"It's because his job is to guard Nightmare Moon's helm," Sweetie Belle realized. "With the peryton trapped, Auntie Eclipse could've already stolen it!"

"We have to find her and stop her," Apple Bloom told the creature. "Can you help us?"

The peryton's eyes glowed with white intensity, and it sniffed the air. It reared and raced down the corridor, its hoof-claws chiming a rhythm.

"What does *that* mean?" Scootaloo asked.

"Follow me!" Sweetie Belle translated. The Crusaders raced after the charging creature, following it down the hallway toward a slab-blocked door. With a powerful kick of its front hooves, the peryton cracked the stone blocking the exit, then used its massive antlers to hurl aside the chunks of broken rock.

"We *never* would've gotten out of here without Smartyhoof," Scootaloo observed.

"I bet Lilymoon and Ambermoon knew that! That's why they left us that drawin' and all those arrows as clues! They're secretly helpin' us!" Apple Bloom said, grinning at her friends' cleverness.

The peryton paused to make sure the Crusaders were following it, then led the way through the doorframe and down another long moss-lit passage.

"But how did Lilymoon and Ambermoon escape Auntie's mind-control spell?" Sweetie Belle wondered as the Crusaders trotted after the peryton. "The last time we saw them, they followed her orders to attack us."

"Maybe Lumi Nation freed them," Scootaloo reminded her friends. "Blue Moon said the two of them tried to protect their daughters from Auntie when they could, remember?"

"Right!" Apple Bloom agreed. "And it's not like Auntie needs 'em anymore now that she got 'em to open the Livewood for her."

The peryton chimed what almost sounded like an *ahem*. The Crusaders looked up to see it was blocking the passage ahead with its body. It tossed its horns toward a vine-covered section of wall.

"What does it want us to do now?" Scootaloo wondered.

"Smartyhoof, are those vines important?" Sweetie Belle asked. Bells answered her. "You want us to look at them?" Sweetie Belle continued. More bells. Answering yes-or-no questions could take forever, Apple Bloom realized, and they didn't have much time to catch up to Auntie. So she trotted over to the vine-covered wall and put her hoof to it. The wall slid smoothly aside.

"*Oh!* You want us to *touch* the wall," Sweetie Belle said, finally figuring out what the peryton was trying to say.

"Yeah, I think we got that," Scootaloo

commented wryly, pointing to Apple Bloom. Sweetie Belle looked over to see the open passage and blushed sheepishly. The peryton chimed a laugh and led the way through the passage.

Inside, the corridor was dark without much moss to light the way. The air was damp, and the smell of wet earth tickled Apple Bloom's nose. She sneezed.

The ground began to slope down, and the path widened. Ahead, Apple Bloom could see a huge cavern, colorful stalactites stretching from the ceiling to try to meet thick, striped stalagmites that lined the ground.

The peryton began to slowly, gingerly pick its way through the stalagmites. Apple Bloom tripped over one, accidentally bumping into Scootaloo, who jostled Sweetie Belle. With an *"Oof,"* the three Crusaders rolled to a very bumpy stop.

"How about we walk on an actual *path*?" Scootaloo said, pointing a wing at a smooth track that ran down the middle of the cavern, brightly lit by the warm glow of the moss.

"My bruises agree with you," Sweetie Belle said, rubbing a hoof against her flank. Apple Bloom grinned and trotted toward the path, her friends following her.

Behind them came the clanging of alarmed bells.

"It's okay, Smartyhoof! We're just moving out here so we can see where we're going." Sweetie Belle reassured the peryton as the three Crusaders stepped on the path.

As soon as their hooves touched the path, the ground beneath them sank.

"It's another trap!" Apple Bloom realized, leaping back off the path. But it was too late. Sweetie Belle and Scootaloo stumbled backward next to her as black slime oozed up through the walkway.

"That is so *gross*!" Scootaloo screwed up her face in disgust. Almost as if it heard her, the glistening slime extended sticky tendrils, whipping out and attaching itself to the Crusaders' hooves. It tugged at the three fillies, trying to pull them into the growing pool of black liquid bubbling from beneath the path.

"The time pocket!" Apple Bloom yelled. Scootaloo tried to reach for her satchel but another tendril snaked up and stuck to her hoof.

"I can't reach it!" she screamed.

Hooves chiming, the peryton leaped to join the Crusaders. It buffeted them with its shadowy wings, knocking them free of the sticky tentacles and sending them rolling off the path in different directions. But when it tried to fly to safety, it was too late! The ooze enveloped its clawed hind feet, pulling it toward the bubbling black pool in the ground. It reared and fought, bells chiming its fear.

"Smartyhoof!" Sweetie Belle yelled. But the peryton was swallowed by the dark muck, bells fading into silence.

A massive river of black ichor spewed up through the path, splitting the cavern in two. The whole cave shook, crumbling around the Cutie Mark Crusaders. Stalactites crashed around Apple Bloom, separating her from her friends. She peered between them to see Sweetie Belle on her right, taking shelter in a narrow crack in the wall. On her left, Scootaloo was ducking and dodging as she ran for a side passage.

Then the ground below Apple Bloom opened, and she suddenly found herself sliding into nothingness. She screamed into the oncoming darkness.

CHAPTER SEVEN

Scootaloo planted her back hooves, flapped her wings, and shoved with all her might.

But the exit was well and truly blocked. The pile of rubble that had fallen in the cavern's collapse wouldn't budge. She was separated from her friends and stuck in this side passage. Unless...

Scootaloo rummaged in her bag and grabbed the time pocket.

"I want a do-over!" she commanded. Nothing happened. She shook the golden artifact fiercely. "Come on, come on! Activate!" It was no use. The time pocket took Unicorn magic to activate. The thing was just a fancy paperweight in Scootaloo's hooves. Why hadn't she given it to Sweetie Belle to carry?

"Fine!" Scootaloo said with more bravado than she felt. "I didn't want to go back that way anyhow." It wasn't true, but saying it made her feel like she was somehow taking charge of things. She turned away from the blocked exit and continued down the narrow passage, trying not to think about how it might be leading her farther away from her friends... or toward Auntie Eclipse.

The passageway wound in a slow curve before opening into a large room, lined with... Scootaloo blinked. Blue flowers? *How does anything grow this far underground?* Scootaloo wondered. Even odder, the flowers were in evenly spaced decorative pots, about a pony apart. What were they doing here? Who planted them? Had she stumbled on a long-forgotten flower shop? Scootaloo trotted over to examine one of the pots more closely. Blue bulbs sprouted several stamens, with large leaves striped with darker blue. Scootaloo frowned. There was something familiar about those flowers....

And then she remembered them. Poison Joke! If anypony came in contact with that, the plant would magically turn the pony's abilities or personality into a cruel practical joke. Good thing she'd recognized it—that was close.

"As long as I don't touch any of them, I'll be fine..." Scootaloo reassured herself, slowly edging around the nearest pot.

Suddenly, the flowers closest to her whipped out dark roots that grabbed for her flank. Scootaloo dodged in the nick of time.

"Unless they try to touch me!" she yelped, twisting as another set of wicked roots snapped out toward her. She ducked and dodged, but the plants were everywhere! As soon as she twirled away from one set of grasping leaves, a snapping flower tried to catch her wing. It was no use—the plants were everywhere! You'd have to be the fastest pony in Equestria to get past these! Fortunately, Scootaloo happened to know that pony. And she'd trained by Rainbow Dash's side for a moment just like this.

Narrowing her eyes, Scootaloo prepared to run the most dangerous obstacle course of her life. With a yell, she raced into the maze of menacing pots.

CHAPTER EIGHT

Apple Bloom bucked the rocky wall next to her in frustration. High above, she could see the opening that led back to where she'd been separated from her friends, but it was impossible to reach. Even if she *could* find a safe path along the rocky outcroppings that lined the walls of her prison, there was *no* way to crawl along the ceiling and get out the way she came in.

"*Sweetie Belle! Scootaloo!* Can y'all hear me?" The only response Apple Bloom got was the echoing of her own voice. She was definitely on her own.

She studied the cave walls. Stones and boulders of all shapes and sizes jutted out at different angles. Thankfully, they were covered with the glowing purple moss just like the caverns above. She hopped onto the nearest rock and tested how sturdy it was. When she was satisfied it was secure, she began leaping from rock to rock. She couldn't get out the way she fell in, but maybe there was some other path hidden out of sight somewhere she could try.

Something clattered along the cave floor.

"Sweetie Belle? Scootaloo?" Apple Bloom thought it sounded like somepony had knocked over a wooden chair. But why would there be a chair in the cave?

She heard the sound again. But it went on longer this time. Like the wooden chair was rolling down a hill.

"Lilymoon? Ambermoon?" Apple Bloom *really* hoped whatever was making that sound was a pony.

Something hissed. Apple Bloom scrambled up to a higher outcropping and hid behind a large boulder. The clattering was constant now. Apple Bloom gulped. This was *definitely* not a pony. She wished her friends were there. This was usually the moment where Scootaloo said something that sounded brave. Or Sweetie Belle would make a joke about being scared and Apple Bloom would comfort her. Without them around to play off, Apple Bloom felt lost. She had *no* idea what to do. She was really on her own.

What would Applejack do if she *were here right now?* Apple Bloom wondered. When she closed her eyes, she could almost *hear* her sister talking to her.

First off, take a breath, she would say. Apple Bloom took a breath. *Ya don't even know what it is yer dealin' with. Once you see it, I'm bettin' it won't be near as scary as it sounds*. Apple Bloom nodded to herself. That seemed like good advice. She peeked around the boulder.

It was *way* scarier than it sounded. It was made out of logs and vines wrapped together, just like a Timberwolf. But it was *much* bigger. It had no legs, so the logs along the bottom rolled over the cave floor, making that loud clattering-chair noise. The logs continued up the body until they reached the large flat head, which held two glowing-green slit pupil eyes. They seemed to study the cave walls, searching. The creature's mouth opened, revealing sharp jagged slivers of wood for teeth. A long vine slithered out of its mouth, tasting the air.

Apple Bloom was trapped in a cave with a giant Timbersnake.

CHAPTER NINE

Sweetie Belle stood alone in the rubble, unsure of what to do. Everything had happened so fast. Beyond the river of black goo, a rocky chasm yawned. Apple Bloom was down there somewhere, hopefully okay. On the other side of the cavern was the side tunnel Scootaloo had raced down to avoid the falling debris. Unfortunately, a pile of broken stalactites was now blocking the pathway. Sweetie Belle couldn't jump across the river to try to find Apple Bloom. Her magic wasn't strong enough to clear the path and follow Scootaloo. That left...

"Smartyhoof," she breathed. It was their fault the peryton had been grabbed by that... slime pond. Maybe there was still something she could do to help. Sweetie Belle made her way carefully over to the now-still pool of ooze, keeping a safe distance. She levitated a small rock and tossed it into the pit. It landed with a *plop* and slowly sunk. Nothing.

Feeling a bit bolder, Sweetie Belle shot a small bolt of magic at the slime pond. A slimy tentacle whipped out of the water and snaked toward her. A shimmering green shield of magic appeared in the air in front of her, blocking the ooze. Sweetie Belle whispered a silent thanks to Twilight for teaching her that move!

"Are you *trying* to get stuck in there?" a voice behind Sweetie Belle asked. Sweetie Belle spun around... to find Lumi Nation. She stood on top of a pile of debris, studying Sweetie Belle with an unreadable expression.

"Stay back!" Sweetie Belle warned, but then remembered that Lumi had been trying to protect her daughters, just like Blue Moon.

"Unless you're good. I'm *really* confused right now. Are you still under Auntie Eclipse's spell? Or did you break it like Blue Moon?" At the sound of her husband's name, Lumi's expression changed. She suddenly looked tired, worried, and... hopeful?

"Is Blue all right? You've seen him?" Lumi asked, eyes wide.

"He's fine. He's with Twilight and the others. He told us everything," Sweetie Belle explained, still wary.

"Thank Celestia he's safe." Lumi heaved a sigh of relief, and her facade of strength seemed to crumble.

"We know you both were Auntie Eclipse's prisoners," Sweetie Belle added tentatively. "Um... are you still following her orders?"

"She sent me and my daughters to stop you three, while she gets the helm," Lumi said, and Sweetie Belle took a step backward. "But I am not here to harm you," Lumi continued quickly. "We must find my daughters, free them, and stop that evil sorceress together. I'm so sorry for everything. I had lost all hope that we would ever be free from Auntie Eclipse. It wasn't until you fillies started to get in her way that I began to believe we could possibly escape her."

Sweetie Belle grinned. It was really nice to know she and her friends could make such a difference. But then she looked back at the pond. They couldn't help everypony. Lumi followed her gaze.

"Are the others stuck in the slumberslime?" she asked with genuine concern.

"Slumberslime?" Sweetie Belle had never heard of that. "Not them. It's Smartyhoof. The peryton."

"The peryton!" Lumi seemed surprised. "But Auntie Eclipse trapped it. That's how she got into the Livewood, once we opened the vine gate. Nopony without a matching cutie mark can enter, unless they travel with the peryton."

"We freed him from that horrible box! But then he got stuck again. Because of us." She frowned. But then she looked up at Lumi hopefully. "Unless you know how to get him out?"

Lumi craned her neck, regarding the pool of slime. "Slumberslime places you into a deep sleep and keeps you that way indefinitely. Only something deeply personal can wake you and give you the strength to free yourself. A memory, a favorite story..."

"A song?" Sweetie Belle asked hopefully.

Lumi shrugged. "It's certainly worth a try." Sweetie Belle took a few steps closer to the slumberslime and cleared her throat. She hoped this worked!

"A rose has thorns to keep it safe, but ponies have not one," Sweetie Belle sang. As she did, the slime in the pond began to bubble. *"A wild rose blooms where it is placed, but ponies seek the sun."* She heard a faint jingling. *"A rose is sweet and beautiful; its scent is lush and rare. But a pony's love is greater yet, and nothing can compare."* A large shape rose up from the center of the pond and, encouraged, Sweetie Belle sang louder. *"So if I had to choose between a rose and pony friend, I'd throw away the flower quick and keep you till the end."* Sweetie Belle finished the song, and the slime melted away from the figure. The peryton leaped out of the slumberslime, and the jingling of bells reverberated through the chamber!

"Wakey wakey!" Sweetie Belle giggled. The peryton nuzzled the young Unicorn gratefully. Then it saw Lumi Nation and leaped in front of Sweetie Belle protectively, pawing the ground. Lumi backed away, but Sweetie Belle rushed forward.

"No, no! It's okay, Smartyhoof! She's good now. She helped us save you twice!"

"Twice?" Lumi asked, confused.

"Here and before, with the drawings on the wall," Sweetie Belle clarified.

"Drawings!" Recognition bloomed in Lumi's eyes. "I think there's something I need to show you." She turned and began trotting away.

"But my friends!" Sweetie Belle protested.

Lumi looked over her shoulder. "Trust me, I have a feeling I know right where you can find them."

CHAPTER TEN

If only the Wonderbolts could see me now, Scootaloo thought. Flipping, flapping, rolling, dodging, she raced past the Poison Joke's snares with a speed and style that would've impressed even the stoic Spitfire. Snarls of roots and stalks whipped out, catching only the air Scootaloo had been in a moment before. Panting, she mustered her strength for one last charge. It would take nearly the speed of a Sonic Rainboom to pull this off. . . .

Flapping her wings into a blur, Scootaloo leaped high, kicked off the corner of a pot, and flung herself into the air. The breeze of the grasping blue tendrils ruffled her mane, but nothing touched her as she spun like an airborne top, zooming forward. . . .

Scootaloo skid-crashed to a landing and rolled over a few times, blinking up at the rocky roof of the cave . . . past the reach of the Poison Joke plants. She'd done it! Scootaloo laughed and punched the air with a hoof.

"And *that's* how Pegasi do it!" she yelled triumphantly. Suddenly, a blast of magic struck the ground next to her, and Scootaloo yelped.

Leaping to her feet, she looked over to see Ambermoon approaching. The Unicorn's face was twisted in a cruel grin that left no question in Scootaloo's mind—her friend was still under Auntie Eclipse's magical control. Scootaloo raised a hoof and began to slowly back away.

"Hey, Ambermoon. You don't want to do this; trust me!" The Poison Joke roots reached for Scootaloo, and she stopped backing up. She was trapped.

Ambermoon didn't answer. Instead, she charged. Scootaloo hoped her friend would forgive her for what happened next, because Scootaloo couldn't stop Ambermoon, but she knew something else that could. Scootaloo stood her ground as long as possible, then tucked and rolled to the side. Ambermoon couldn't stop her forward momentum fast enough, and she crashed headlong into a Poison Joke plant.

Scootaloo watched, holding her breath, as the Unicorn sat up, her eyes clearing, a strange look on her face.

"Ambermoon? You okay?"

Ambermoon gave a silly giggle and suddenly *bounced* out of the flowers. Scootaloo gaped. Her friend's legs now ended in blue springs, not hooves!

"Come on in, Scootaloo!" Ambermoon singsonged as she pogoed around the room.

Scootaloo frowned, but then it all made sense. Ambermoon was one of the most serious, rigid ponies she knew. Of course the Poison Joke's prank on her would be to turn her silly and bouncy.

"Riiight," Scootaloo said placatingly as Ambermoon ricocheted off the walls, laughing hysterically. "Why don't we go see if we can find the rest of our friends, and save the bounce party for later?"

Ambermoon wasn't listening. Instead, she was batting one of her springs to her lips, making a *boing-boing-boing* noise and giggling at it.

"I hear there's a super-springy floor of cheese this way," Scootaloo said temptingly, trying to think of the most random thing she could.

It worked. Ambermoon flipped out of the Poison Joke plants. Her mane had gone even frizzier than Pinkie Pie's, and she bounced ahead happily.

"Last one there is a rotten cockatrice egg!" the now-goofy Unicorn sang. Scootaloo shrugged and followed. She had no idea how they were going to find Sweetie Belle and Apple Bloom in this maze of traps and tunnels . . . but at least Ambermoon wasn't trying to attack her anymore.

CHAPTER ELEVEN

Apple Bloom wished she had *never* wanted to go on adventures like Applejack. She wished she had *never* followed Lilymoon into the forest after that bogle. She wished she were in the Crusader Clubhouse with Sweetie Belle and Scootaloo, discussing who needed help understanding their cutie mark.

Now, hang on, Applejack said in her head. *After all you've been through, I know you can handle this!* But Apple Bloom realized that what Scootaloo had said earlier was true. They'd *always* had help from somepony else. At the *very* least, Apple Bloom always had her friends with her. She couldn't do this alone! *You ain't never alone*, Applejack said. *I'll always be there, Sugarcube.* Even though Apple Bloom knew it was just the sister in her head, it still made her feel a little better.

The Timbersnake's tongue flickered right above the boulder where Apple Bloom was hiding. She didn't move. She didn't even breathe. The tongue disappeared. After a few seconds, the clacking of the creature's wooden body faded as it moved to the side of the cavern where it had come from.

Where it had come from! It had to have come from *somewhere*. Maybe that somewhere led back to her friends! Apple Bloom knew she needed to act while the snake was searching the far side of the cave. She took a deep breath and *slowly* crept around the boulder. The large serpent's back was to her as it studied a pile of rocks. She *quietly* jumped down the boulders and looked over her shoulder. The Timbersnake wasn't paying her any attention. She snuck in the opposite direction, scanning the walls for an opening large enough for the wooden beast.

There! She had missed it at first because there was a giant stone blocking it, but now she could see there was a tunnel out of the cave, and it looked like it was going up! Apple Bloom risked running a little faster.

Something walked out of the shadows, blocking her way. Wait, not something. Somepony!

It was Lilymoon!

Apple Bloom was thrilled! Not only had she left them clues, but here was her friend, ready to help her find her way out of the cave! Apple Bloom saw Lilymoon's horn shine bright with magic. Apple Bloom wasn't sure what she was doing, but she hoped it wouldn't attract—

Lilymoon blasted a bolt of magic at Apple Bloom. She was attacking her! And worse, the noise attracted the Timbersnake, whose large head whipped around at the sound of the blast!

"Lilymoon! Stop it! You're gonna turn us into Timbersnake chow!" Apple Bloom said as loud as she dared, barreling into her friend, knocking her to the ground.

Apple Bloom could hear the snake clattering toward them, hissing angrily. Her friend still had that blank expression on her face, the same one as her father. It had taken a blast of magic from Starlight to break Blue Moon free of the spell. Not an option for Apple Bloom.

Lilymoon stood, powering up her horn once again. Apple Bloom needed to break that spell and she needed to do it fast. If only there were a way to get Lilymoon to blast *herself* with magic . . . Desperate, Apple Bloom leaped at Lilymoon.

"This is gonna hurt me way more than it's gonna hurt you!" Apple Bloom said.

Lilymoon's horn released a bolt of magic. But Apple Bloom was so close, the spell exploded around *both* of them in a flash of light. They hit the ground in a tangle of hooves. Apple Bloom groaned; that was a real whammy.

Lilymoon groaned next to her. She sat up, shaking her head back and forth. She turned to Apple Bloom.

"Apple Bloom?" Lilymoon asked, looking around in confusion. "Where are we?" A hissing behind them reminded Apple Bloom they weren't out of danger yet. She grabbed her friend by the hoof, pulling her up.

"In a cave with a giant Timbersnake. So how about we save explanations till after the daring escape?" Lilymoon looked behind Apple Bloom, and her eyes widened. The

Timbersnake had spotted them, and it was clattering quickly toward them. Narrowing her eyes, Lilymoon shot a blast of magic straight up at the ceiling. There was a loud explosion, and several large rocks fell between the ponies and the snake, blocking the ferocious wooden monster. Apple Bloom grinned at her friend.

"Nice to have you back on our side," she said to Lilymoon.

"Nice to *be* back," Lilymoon agreed. And the two of them hurried off to find the others.

CHAPTER TWELVE

After reaching several dead ends in the Livewood's maze of passages, Apple Bloom was relieved when she and Lilymoon came across a tall staircase in the cavern ahead. Seemingly grown from twisted roots, it curled in a spiral up into darkness.

"Finally, somethin' goin' the way we want!" Apple Bloom said. "Up!" Hopefully the stairway would lead them back to the level where she'd left the other Crusaders. Apple Bloom stepped onto the strange stairs, and Lilymoon followed. The roots under their hooves were slippery and dry. The higher they got, the harder Apple Bloom found it to keep her balance on the narrow, curving walkway. The roots seemed to sway under their steps, and Apple Bloom tried not to look at the dizzying fall below. Then suddenly, the stairs began to move. Lilymoon gasped as the roots beneath their hooves began to unbraid. The stairway was coming apart—with them on it!

"It must be a trap! Hurry, Lilymoon!" Apple Bloom cried, scrambling upward as fast as she could. It was no use. With a loud rip, the roots parted, and both ponies plummeted toward the ground below! Apple Bloom shut her eyes and screamed.

Suddenly, a rush of wings filled Apple Bloom's ears, along with a cheerful chiming. She wasn't falling anymore; she was . . . flying?

Apple Bloom looked down to see that the peryton was carrying her on its back. Nearby, Lumi Nation gently lowered Lilymoon to the ground with her magic. Sweetie Belle raced over and hugged her friend as Apple Bloom slid off Smartyhoof's back.

"You're all right!" she yelled. Apple Bloom hugged her friend back, grateful to see she was okay, too. Then, glancing around the room, she realized somepony was missing.

"Where's Scootaloo?" Apple Bloom asked. Sweetie Belle shook her head.

"I don't know, but if Ambermoon's with her, Lumi Nation should be able to find them," Sweetie Belle explained. "She's on our side now." But before Apple Bloom could ask more questions, the ground shook with a strange noise. Apple Bloom looked in the direction of the sound. It came again and again, the ground shaking with each odd *sproing*. Apple Bloom held her breath. Was it another trap?

"Surprise!" came a cheery voice. And suddenly, Ambermoon leaped out of the shadows, landing with a bouncy *sproing* that shook the cavern. Apple Bloom gasped. The

pony's mane and tail were spun out like purple cotton candy, and her hooves were... *springs*? Scootaloo raced in after Ambermoon, panting.

"She's... really... fast on those things," Scootaloo gasped.

"What happened?" Sweetie Belle asked, eyeing Ambermoon as she giggled to herself, doing bouncy flips in place.

"It looks like a bad case of Poison Joke." Lumi Nation frowned. The Unicorn stepped forward, producing a vial of antidote. "The smallest touch can affect a pony, which is why when Blue Moon started growing it for Auntie's use, I always made sure to have the antidote nearby." Lumi trotted over to Ambermoon and drenched her with the curative potion.

Ambermoon blinked, her mane and tail falling back into their normal style. With a magical *poof*, the springs at the end of her legs became hooves again.

"How do you feel, Ambermoon?" asked Lilymoon, smothering a smile as she looked at her sister.

Ambermoon scowled back. "You better not tell *anypony* about this. Ever."

Apple Bloom grinned. Ambermoon was obviously back to her old self.

"Now that everypony is accounted for, let me show you what I was talking about," Lumi said as a magical globe of light materialized in front of her. "This is why I assumed we would all end up meeting here." The globe of light floated along the path ahead, its glow revealing a wall mural similar to the one the Crusaders had encountered earlier. This one also had crude drawings of each of the Crusaders, but, in addition, there were three Unicorns who broadly resembled

Ambermoon, Lilymoon, and Lumi Nation. Above them was an outline of the peryton with cute little bells drawn around his antlers.

"So you *did* leave us those clues!" Apple Bloom grinned at the Moon family.

Ambermoon and Lilymoon looked confused. Lumi Nation shook her head.

"We didn't draw these," Ambermoon said, sharing a look with her sister. "We thought you could tell us what they mean."

"We don't know, either. We figured you guys were leaving us clues." Scootaloo cocked her head. "If *you* didn't draw them . . . who did?" All the ponies turned to look at the peryton, but he snorted and shook his antlers back and forth.

"That's definitely a no," Sweetie Belle translated.

"Whoever created these must've wanted to help," Lumi Nation said, sending the floating orb of light down the hall, revealing more arrows drawn on the walls. "The arrows seem to avoid all the traps in these passages. They're as good a guide as any."

Apple Bloom frowned—somepony had to have left the drawings and clues. And something told her that it was important to figure out who. But it would have to wait. Right now, they had to stop Auntie Eclipse from becoming the next Nightmare Moon.

CHAPTER THIRTEEN

"There," Lumi Nation said, stopping in front of an ornate gateway taller than twenty ponies. Apple Bloom could see the stone doors were etched with two Alicorns—Princess Luna and Princess Celestia. Their horns were crossed, and the warning was clear—this was a place nopony should enter.

"The helm must be in there," Sweetie Belle breathed. Beside her, the peryton chimed an affirmative answer.

"What do you want us to do?" Lumi asked, turning to the Cutie Mark Crusaders. "What is your plan?"

Apple Bloom considered that. They didn't really have a plan besides "save the day," which, when you said it aloud, sounded kind of unprepared.

"We haven't really thought it all out yet," Scootaloo admitted.

Okay, really *unprepared*, Apple Bloom amended.

"We'll focus on gettin' the helm," Apple Bloom said, "if you four can keep Auntie distracted."

Ambermoon looked skeptically at Lilymoon. "Not much can distract her when she really wants something," the older Unicorn said.

"She would move the heavens, Equestria, and time itself to get that helm," Lumi said. "But somehow, you three always manage to surprise her."

"Mother means that we believe in you," Lilymoon said to Apple Bloom. "There's a reason we're all in this together. And if anypony can stop Auntie, it's you."

Apple Bloom was warmed by her friend's

earnest words. She looked to Sweetie Belle, who nodded, and Scootaloo, who stomped a determined hoof. They were ready for whatever waited behind those door—

CRASH! The stone doors *flew* off the wall in a burst of bloodred magic. The ponies and peryton ducked, hitting the floor as shards of carved marble flew past. A horrible laugh rang out around them. Apple Bloom looked up and saw they were too late. Auntie Eclipse was wearing Nightmare Moon's helm.

The ancient Unicorn had become a jet-black Alicorn. Her mane seemed to contain the entire night sky, stars twinkling in its depths as it flowed in an unseen breeze. She was taller, younger, and practically glowing with evil power.

Heh. Even the biggest apples fall in the right wind, Applejack seemed to say in Apple Bloom's head. Apple Bloom wished the advice were a tad more specific, but it would have to do.

"Now!" Apple Bloom yelled. And around her, her companions leaped into action. The peryton flew at Auntie Eclipse, while Sweetie Belle and Scootaloo moved to either side.

As one, Lumi Nation, Ambermoon, and Lilymoon lowered their horns and blasted magic at the sorceress.

But Auntie summoned a shield of light that flew from her horn like a battering ram. The peryton was hurled into the shadows, bells jangling as it landed heavily. The Moon family was blown backward, sliding to their knees. Lumi grimaced and forced herself back up on her hooves. Auntie didn't wait for her to recover. She hurled another spell, this one crackling up a wall of flame around her in a circle, keeping Lumi, Ambermoon, Lilymoon, and the peryton at bay. Apple Bloom winced at the sudden heat. The Crusaders were trapped inside the ring of fire with Auntie, which on one hoof was good news... but on the other, super dangerous.

Apple Bloom dodged around Auntie's flank, just like they'd practiced with Twilight. Sweetie Belle used a burst of magic to lift Apple Bloom skyward, and she kicked her rear hooves out with all her might at Auntie's helm... but a shudder of icy magic froze the Crusaders in place!

"You pitiful fools! No filly is stopping me from my destiny!" Auntie Eclipse roared.

Apple Bloom struggled to free herself from her pose in midair, but her efforts sent her crashing to the ground on her side, still frozen.

Is this it? Apple Bloom thought wildly. After everypony believing in them, was this how the whole adventure ended? She tried to look at her friends, but all she could see was the painting on the wall she faced. Wait. The painting?

It was an image of the time pocket. Well, a lot of images, actually. The time pocket was painted over and over again on the wall. It had to be some kind of sign. Apple Bloom wanted to cry. Of course they could use the time pocket . . . if they could reach it! But nopony in the ring of fire could move. She wished they could have as many do-overs as the paintings on the wall. She noticed something else. In the corner was a drawing of a big apple falling from a tree. It looked as if the artist had drawn a gust of wind knocking it down. No, that wasn't it exactly. It wasn't wind. There was an Earth pony wearing a bow. The wind was coming from her mouth. It was *laughter*! An apple falling from a tree was exactly what Applejack's voice in Apple Bloom's head had just said! It was as if the mysterious artist could hear what she was thinking.

And then it hit her. She knew who left the clues. And if she was right, she knew exactly how to beat Auntie Eclipse!

"Now all of Equestria and beyond will bow to my might!" Auntie Eclipse crowed with wicked glee.

"Good luck with that!" Apple Bloom said. She was grateful the spell freezing her didn't extend to her voice. Auntie Eclipse whirled on Apple Bloom, eyes burning in rage.

"What was that, you little worm?"

"Oh, nothin'. Just not sure how you're gonna get all of Equestria to bow to ya when you can't even stop three fillies from messin' up your plans. You're pretty bad at this, Auntie."

"Don't call me that!" the evil Alicorn raged. "My new name is Eclipse Destiny!"

Apple Bloom burst out laughing.

"Uh-oh. She's lost it," Apple Bloom heard Scootaloo say from somewhere behind her.

"All this time to plan and that's the best name you could come up with?" Apple Bloom chuckled. Auntie Eclipse seethed in anger.

"Apple Bloom!" Sweetie Belle hissed. "*Why are you making her angrier?*"

"Silence!" Eclipse Destiny boomed. "You may have been a thorn in my side before, but that ends *now*."

"You mean you don't wanna know *how* we've always been one step ahead of you? Apple Bloom asked sweetly, laying her trap. Eclipse Destiny paused.

"What do you mean?" She frowned.

Got her, Apple Bloom thought. "Princess Luna and Princess Celestia gave us all the magic we need to beat you!" she boasted.

"What is she—?" Sweetie Belle began, but thankfully Scootaloo shushed her.

"Ah, I see what your plan is. To try to distract me to buy time." The sorceress smiled craftily. "If you're so powerful, by all means, use this amazing magic to stop me."

"It ain't like that. We're protected. If you use the helm's magic against us, it will go to you instead!" Apple Bloom was making this up as she went along, but she thought it *sounded* good at least. She peered around the cavern until she saw an area swathed in shadows. This was the moment of truth. She really hoped this worked. "If you don't believe me, just look at that wall over there!"

"What are you talking ab—" Eclipse Destiny turned toward the shadowy area and gawked, confused. Painted on the wall was an image of a powerful, angry-looking Alicorn. She was blasting three young fillies with magic but they had lines drawn around them, protecting them. The magic bounced back from the barrier in a blast of wavy lines that made it clear the Alicorn was the one in trouble.

"Whoa," Scootaloo and Sweetie Belle both whispered behind Apple Bloom.

"What? *What trickery is this?!*" Eclipse Destiny snarled, but there was doubt in her voice now, Apple Bloom was sure.

"It's no trick, Auntie. Haven't you heard?" Apple Bloom asked. "Friendship is Magic. And we've got some pretty powerful friends!" Now for the most dangerous, most important part of her plan. Apple Bloom tried to sound as confident as Rainbow Dash, putting a mocking tone in her voice as she needled the evil Alicorn further. "As long as you wear that helm, you can't hurt us! If you try, the danger will come back at you a hundred times stronger!" Apple Bloom was close enough to see Eclipse Destiny's eyes darting bath and forth, clearly unsure of what she should do. Apple Bloom held her breath—would the sorceress fall for it? Then Eclipse Destiny smiled.

"Foolish child. I have plenty of magic even without this artifact." Nightmare Moon's helm lifted from Eclipse Destiny's head, and the terrifying Alicorn transformed back into the slightly-less-terrifying Auntie Eclipse. Auntie grinned craftily at Apple Bloom. "I'll use my *own* magic to destroy you, and then regain the helm's power once agai—"

A powerful blast of magic blew through the ring of fire and hurled Auntie Eclipse back against the wall. Suddenly, Apple Bloom could move again, and the blaze surrounding her and her friends faded to ash. She turned her head to see Lumi Nation, Ambermoon, and Lilymoon standing together, horns glowing brightly. They had hit Auntie Eclipse with a triple whammy!

"That's for... well... *everything*!" Lilymoon said, glaring at the unconscious old witch.

CHAPTER FOURTEEN

"There," Lumi Nation said, nodding her head in approval. "That should hold her temporarily." If Apple Bloom didn't know how powerful Auntie Eclipse was, she would have thought all the shields, bindings, spells, and curses Lumi and her daughters had cast around the Unicorn's unconscious form were kinda overdoing it. As it was, Apple Bloom was still nervous that Auntie Eclipse might suddenly wake up. Lumi Nation turned and studied the Cutie Mark Crusaders. "Now... how in the name of Celestia did you do all that?"

Apple Bloom's friends shrugged.

"We were just as confused as you were!" Sweetie Belle said.

"*More* confused," Scootaloo corrected.

"Didn't y'all think those drawin's everywhere looked familiar?" Apple Bloom asked, grinning. Scootaloo glanced at the wall behind them.

"I guess?" she said, clearly unsure where Apple Bloom was going.

"Think back to our Clubhouse," Apple Bloom prodded. Sweetie Belle's eyes widened.

"The drawings look like Crusader checklists!" she squealed. Apple Bloom nodded.

"I finally figured out who was leavin' those clues along the way. *We* were leavin' 'em for ourselves!"

"Say *what*, now?" Scootaloo asked, completely baffled.

"*Somepony* was lookin' out for us and leavin' clues that Auntie Eclipse wouldn't pay much attention to," Apple Bloom explained, walking over to the wall with all the time pockets painted on it. "Once we knew it wasn't Lilymoon, Ambermoon, or Lumi Nation, there weren't a lotta options left. When I saw all these time pockets and this apple tree in the corner, I finally put it together."

"You have Blue Moon's time pocket." Lumi nodded her head in realization. "And you knew you were going to go back in time after this was all over to leave yourselves all the clues you needed!" She smiled. "That's really quite clever."

"Wait. *Wait!*" Scootaloo's face was scrunched up as though she were working on a particularly difficult math problem. "So *later* we are *going to* leave ourselves clues in the *past. Before* we went into the Livewood. So when we *did* enter, we *found* the clues we left ourselves?" Everypony considered that.

"I *think* that's right?" Ambermoon finally said.

"So the drawing of the magic bouncing back on Auntie Eclipse..." Scootaloo said, turning to Apple Bloom. "You just decided in the moment we were gonna go back in time to draw it and it appeared?"

"Yup!" Apple Bloom nodded.

Scootaloo sighed. "I hate time travel."

Suddenly, Auntie Eclipse stirred. All the ponies froze. But Auntie Eclipse gave a sigh and slumped again, still unconscious for the moment.

"It won't take her long to get through all those shields when she wakes up." Lilymoon grimaced, watching her "aunt" warily.

"It won't take her long to get out of *any* prison," Lumi Nation said sadly. "We'll need something powerful to keep her trapped until the princesses decide what to do with her." The group silently considered what could be done when an excited chiming broke through their music. The peryton was prancing in place.

"What is it, Smartyhoof?" Sweetie Belle asked. In response, the peryton leaped over them and galloped off quickly.

"What was *that* about?" Apple Bloom asked. They all shrugged. Moments later, the peryton came rushing back into the room. He dropped something at Sweetie Belle's hooves. She levitated it for everypony to see.

"It's the box Auntie used to trap the peryton!" Lilymoon exclaimed.

"Well, then, it seems only fair that the peryton gets to use it on Auntie Eclipse." Ambermoon grinned wickedly, opening the box. The peryton moved like a shadowy blur, and before Apple Bloom could tell what was happening, the box was closed and Auntie Eclipse was nowhere to be seen! The peryton snorted at the box and trotted around, quite pleased with himself. The ringing bells and chimes went on for quite some time.

"What did he say?" Apple Bloom asked. Sweetie Belle blushed.

"I don't think it's anything I should be repeating."

"Wait!" Scootaloo shouted. She was still trying to wrap her mind around all the time travel business. "The time pocket only goes back a minute! How are we supposed to use it to go back further?"

"That...I dunno," Apple Bloom admitted.

"Well, clearly you *do* accomplish it," Lumi Nation said, nodding toward the drawings on the wall. "So there *must* be some way. Let's see the time pocket." Scootaloo reached into her pack and pulled it out. Lumi reached for it, but the peryton blocked her way, touching the artifact with his muzzle. The time pocket glowed brightly and rose up until it hovered between the peryton's antlers.

"Um. Did you know he could do that?" Scootaloo asked Sweetie Belle.

"Nope. But I have a feeling he can take us exactly *when* we need to go."

The peryton galloped around all of them until it was hard to see anything. The next thing Apple Bloom felt was a sensation like she was falling backward....

CHAPTER FIFTEEN

"And you're *sure* we got everything?" Sweetie Belle asked for what Apple Bloom thought had to be the billionth time. She couldn't blame her friend—working out everything they had to do in the past to make sure they'd be able to defeat Auntie Eclipse in the future was a brainteaser that even Dr. Hooves would have trouble with. Or as Scootaloo put it...

"Time travel is the *worst*!"

Apple Bloom ran down their checklist. They'd painted the picture of the Cutie Mark Crusaders at the end of the stairs into the Livewood. They'd put arrows all throughout the Livewood, marking the right path to guide their future selves, with the help of the peryton to show them where all the labyrinth's traps were. They had drawn the picture of all of them together in the chamber. Apple Bloom had painted the pictures of the time pocket and the apple tree that would give her the idea that would save them all in the future. *And* they had drawn the picture of the Crusaders being protected from Eclipse Destiny's powers. It seemed as if they had left all the clues that they were gonna need to make it through the Livewood!

"There's just one thing I still don't get...." Scootaloo pounded a hoof against her forehead as though trying to knock loose a thought. "What about the extra lock on the Livewood? You know, the pillars outside that the peryton made?"

"The ones that need three matching cutie marks to work?" Apple Bloom asked.

"Right! How did Smartyhoof know to make them for *us*? He hadn't met us yet. Or is that more time travel stuff?" Scootaloo frowned.

"We could ask him," Sweetie Belle said, turning to the peryton. But in reply, Smartyhoof lowered his antlered head to her and gave a single, low chime. *He sounds sad*, Apple Bloom thought. Sweetie Belle must have thought so, too, because she looked worried. "What's wrong, Smartyhoof?"

The peryton reached gently out with a wing and caressed Sweetie Belle's cheek. Then he stepped backward, his hooves ringing a complex, beautiful song.

"What do you mean, 'you'll see us in our dreams'?" Sweetie Belle cried. "We see you right now. You don't have to go!"

The peryton lifted the time pocket in his antlers and spread his wings. The artifact began to whirl in place, spinning in a sparking rainbow of colors. The peryton galloped around them in a tight circle, wings beating. The sound of bells filled their ears. The rainbow of the time pocket's power became a blur that surrounded the six ponies.

"What's happening?!" Scootaloo yelled into the noise and wind.

"Complex magic," Lumi said, teeth gritted. "Hold on!"

The six ponies touched hooves, and the ground seemed to lurch under them. The world spun, and Apple Bloom felt as if she were being turned inside out and backward all at once. She felt as if she were falling.... Falling....

Then, suddenly, the ground rushed up to meet her, and, with a grunt, she landed in a pile of leaves outside the Livewood.

The anxious eyes of Applejack peered down at her.

"Sugarcube? Can you hear me?" cried Applejack.

Apple Bloom answered her by pulling her sister into a hug.

Twilight, Starlight, Pinkie Pie, Rainbow Dash, Rarity, and Fluttershy pushed in to surround the Crusaders, Ambermoon, Lilymoon, and Lumi Nation in a cacophony of questions and relieved exclamations.

"Did you do it?"

"Where's Auntie Eclipse?"

"Darling, your mane is a disaster!"

"I hope you took lotsa pictures!"

"So, what happened?"

Apple Bloom smiled as the rush of the ponies' caring babble surrounded them all. A joyful voice cut through the hubbub.

"Lumi!" Apple Bloom turned to see Blue Moon racing to greet his family. Lumi tearfully touched her horn to his, and Ambermoon and Lilymoon crowded in close.

"We are finally free of the witch." Lumi smiled.

"Look! Their cutie marks!" Scootaloo breathed.

Apple Bloom blinked—Ambermoon's and Lilymoon's flanks were glowing. Their matching cutie marks blurred into new ones—a prism splitting light into a rainbow on Lilymoon's haunches and an oak tree growing from a book on Ambermoon's.

Lilymoon and Ambermoon looked down at their new marks in surprise.

"Those must be their real cutie marks!" Sweetie Belle said. "The ones Auntie hid with their matching ones! I bet they don't even know what they mean!"

"Well, I know a few ponies who can help with that." Apple Bloom grinned at her friends.

"All right, everypony," Twilight called, "let's get back to the castle. Something tells me our young heroes have quite a story to share." Apple Bloom, Sweetie Belle, and Scootaloo grinned.

As the ponies began the long journey out of the Everfree Forest, Applejack moved to Apple Bloom's side.

"I think I owe you an apology," Applejack said slowly. "You are one of the bravest ponies I know. Whenever I try to stop you from doin' somethin' dangerous, it's not 'cause I think you can't. It's 'cause I wanna protect you. But now I see you don't need me for that anymore."

"Actually, I *do* need you," Apple Bloom blurted out. "Without you, I never coulda made it through the Livewood. Or past that Timbersnake. Or Auntie Eclipse. Whenever I got scared or felt like givin' up, I heard your voice in my head. I *know* you believe in me."

A warm smile bloomed on Applejack's face. "You mean that, Sugarcube?" she asked.

Apple Bloom nodded. "I used to be so jealous of you and your friends havin' all the adventures," Apple Bloom confessed. "But then I realized—everything you've been through has taught me all I know. You're the best kinda big sister to have. And I wouldn't trade you for all the adventures in the world."

"So you don't think I'm too bossy?" asked Applejack, a twinkle of humor in her eye.

"You're just the right amount of bossy," Apple Bloom teased back. And together, the sisters turned away from the Livewood.

CHAPTER SIXTEEN

Apple Bloom trotted quietly next to Sweetie Belle and Scootaloo. She usually talked nonstop all the way to school, but not today. Out of the corner of her eye, she could see Sweetie Belle and Scootaloo glancing in her direction. Sweetie Belle nudged Scootaloo.

"Hey, Apple Bloom. Everything okay?" Scootaloo asked. Before Apple Bloom could answer, a familiar voice called to them.

"Morning, everypony!" Lilymoon hurried over to join the trio, Ambermoon trotting along beside her. Apple Bloom still couldn't get over how different they both seemed. In the weeks since they had defeated Auntie Eclipse, the sisters *and* their parents had been hard at work transforming the formerly creepy and foreboding house on Horseshoe Hill into a warm and happy home. They all seemed more relaxed and at ease in Ponyville, like they finally belonged. Blue Moon and Lumi Nation had even started working with Starlight Glimmer to catalog all the magical books and artifacts in Auntie Eclipse's library! It felt like a brand-new day!

"Hey, Crusaders!" Snips yelled as he and Snails trotted past them toward the Schoolhouse. "Your sisters did it again!"

"They're awesome!" Snails added. Apple Bloom sighed. *Some* things never changed. Applejack, Rarity, Rainbow Dash, and the others had just returned from battling a family of chimeras that were ravaging the apple orchards of Appleloosa.

"That must be tough," Ambermoon remarked as Snips and Snails disappeared over the hill in front of them.

"What?" Sweetie Belle asked.

"Being told how great your sisters are, when the three of you just saved all of Equestria." Ambermoon cocked her head thoughtfully. "*And* our family," she added.

"It would be great to tell somepony," Scootaloo said wistfully.

"But it's definitely better that nopony knows about the Livewood." Sweetie Belle shuddered. "*Or* what's inside." Sweetie Belle's eyes widened and she turned to Apple Bloom. "*That's* what's bothering you this morning, isn't it? That nopony knows we're heroes?"

Apple Bloom thought for a minute before turning to her friends. "It's fine," Apple Bloom said simply. "The ponies who matter know. Our families and close friends. And more importantly, we know it. When it really mattered, we did what needed to be done. That's reward enough for me." Scootaloo and

Sweetie Belle shared a look. "What?" Apple Bloom asked.

"You sounded *just* like your older sister just then," Scootaloo said.

"*Exactly* like her," Sweetie Belle added. Apple Bloom considered that and then nodded, a warm smile creeping across her face.

"Y'know, that woulda bothered me a few weeks ago. But now? I kinda think that's the nicest thing y'all ever said to me." Apple Bloom hugged her two best friends in the world. Lilymoon joined in. Ambermoon let out an overdramatic sigh.

"If I join this group hug, can we get on with our day?" The big grin made it clear she wouldn't be *too* upset about it.

"Get over here!" Scootaloo said, grabbing her by the hoof. The three best friends who had helped save Equestria, and the sisters who had learned the value of true friendship, hugged until the ringing from the Ponyville Schoolhouse bell reminded them they had a big day ahead. They rushed to join the other foals and fillies.

"Y'know, I was thinkin' about our *next* Cutie Mark Crusader adventure..." Apple Bloom began casually. The others all groaned. They had had quite enough adventure for the moment. Apple Bloom giggled. She supposed they could just enjoy being young fillies. At least for a little while...

Read another My Little Pony adventure in:

Available now!

Chapter One

On a normal day, Rainbow Dash would have barely noticed the sunlight peeking through the curtains of her bedroom. But this was not a normal day, and this was not her bedroom. At least, it wasn't *anymore.* Rainbow Dash was back in her hometown of Cloudsdale. Instead of nestling into her fluffy cloud duvet back above Ponyville, the blue Pegasus was tucked tightly into the rainbow-patterned sheets of her fillyhood bed. She had a wing cramp. Clearly the bed was much smaller than she'd remembered.

Rainbow Dash yawned and watched as the light made its way across the eclectic array of trophies, ribbons, and relics of her youth that were still in the exact spots they had been years ago when she'd carefully arranged and rearranged them with her tiny hooves. There were so many memories on display!

Rainbow Dash's eyes landed on her bookshelf, where her old stuffed teddy bear, Blue-Blue, sat with his signature blank expression. Rainbow Dash instantly remembered when her mother had given him to her as a reward for being brave through her first dentist appointment. Rainbow Dash then noticed her cloud-rimmed basketball hoop and recalled all the hours she had spent perfecting the perfect shot instead of completing her homework assignments. She never did enjoy studying too much. Only one test had ever mattered to Rainbow Dash—the one to get into the Wonderbolts!

The poster above the hoop was evidence of Rainbow Dash's longstanding devotion to the elite Pegasus flight team. It depicted the renowned Wonderbolt Super Stream in action—wings outspread and racing toward the big finish in the famous "Eye of the Storm" routine. It was a legendary show! Young Rainbow Dash had stared at that poster as she drifted off to sleep each night, dreaming of the day when she, too, would become a Wonderbolt and don the blue-and-yellow flight suit.

Now that her dream had finally come true, Rainbow Dash often found herself visiting locales across Equestria with her team, performing complex routines and thrilling feats to the delight of adoring onlookers. Which was precisely why she was back here at this very moment, in Cloudsdale, in her parents' house.

"Good morning, dearest Dashie-kins!" Windy Whistles burst into the bedroom, carrying a tray of steaming porridge and toast slathered with cloudberry jam. The cup of orange juice sloshed around as Windy practically shook with excitement at hosting her daughter. "I made your favorite brekkie! How's *my* favorite little Wonderbolt feeling today?!"

"I'm, uh—" Rainbow could barely stammer before her dad, Bow Hothoof, popped in behind her mom.

"Is she up yet, dear? Is our champion daughter ready for her big debut in the Wonderbolts' anniversary show—The Loopy Woop Woop?!" He peered over Windy's shoulder with a gigantic smile spreading across his violet face. His rainbow mane poked out in every direction, just like his daughter's.

"Dad, it's *called* the Loop-de-Loop Hoopla." Rainbow Dash sighed with a smirk as she bolted upright in bed. "And I guess I'm up now." She tossed the covers away and began to climb out.

"No, no! Don't move a muscle, missy," Windy urged as she rushed over and tucked her daughter back in, balancing the breakfast tray in an impressive teetering display. "Relax and eat your food. You need to save your energy for the big performance. Everypony in Cloudsdale is coming, and they just can't wait to see you! The girls are even coming—making a whole day of it! Dressing up, seeing the show, then grabbing lunch afterward at the Raindrop Café. Finally, it's *my* turn to show off my daughter. If I hear another thing about Snowfall's daughter, Moon Trotter, and her Snowflake awards, I just don't know!"

"The *giiirls*?" Rainbow groaned. "All of them?" Rainbow's mother was very active in the Cloudsdale Decorative Plate Collecting Club. It sounded tame enough, but when all those mares got together, they could be quite the hoof-ful.

"No, no, of course not." Windy laughed. "That would be ridiculous! Just Snowfall, Blue Skies, Pom Pom, Dew Shine, Sparkle

Showers, Sunny Shores, and . . . Helen." Windy grinned proudly. "Oh! And Barbara."

"Who doesn't love Barbara?" Rainbow Dash laughed nervously and hid her mounting feelings of anxiety by taking a bite of toast. Ever since she'd blown up at her parents for being too supportive at her last Wonderbolts show, Rainbow Dash had made a serious effort to accept their support and praise. She was a lucky pony to have such loving parents, even if they were over-the-top sometimes. Thanks to Scootaloo and her school report, Rainbow Dash remembered that now.

"And I hope it's okay that I invited the old buckball team, too," Bow Hothoof added, blushing. "They still can't believe that the little tyke who used to fly around the court following 'em and asking 'em to race is a real Wonderbolt now!" Bow wiped away a proud tear. He gathered Rainbow Dash into a big bear hug.

"Invite the whole city, if ya want. I actually invited some friends, too," Rainbow Dash admitted. "But I'm really not sure if they're going to come. I mean—I don't even know if they got my invitation...."

"Why wouldn't they?" Windy furrowed her brow. "Didn't you have their addresses?"

"It's not really like that," Rainbow explained, taking the last bite of porridge. She wiped away a rogue drop from her chin. "They, uh...don't have addresses. These friends are sort of...always on the go? I hope it's okay—I kinda invited them to the house first."

"How lovely!" Windy chirped with her signature optimism. "It's so nice to have guests."

"Well, I can't wait to meet 'em," Bow Hothoof commented. "Any friend of my daughter's is welcome in this home. Now, how about you let me do a bit of tidying before they arrive?" He trotted over to the window and thrust the curtains open. A blast of fresh air and sunlight filled the room. But before Rainbow Dash could thank her dad, Bow let out a loud, startled grunt.

"Whoa!" Bow's jaw dropped and his eyes became larger than a set of Windy Whistle's collector plates. "What in the cumulonimbus is that?!"

"Stand back!" Rainbow Dash sprang to action and darted over. She was ready to take on whatever fearsome sight she might discover. Rainbow Dash wasn't afraid. She'd seen it all: Dragons, Manticores, new and scary creatures in Klugetown, and even a Storm King.

That's why Rainbow Dash should have expected to see the massive object lurching straight toward their house.

But it took her completely by surprise.